TEMPORARY INSANITY

Call in the Calvary

George Clark

authorHOUSE®

AuthorHouse™
1663 Liberty Drive
Bloomington, IN 47403
www.authorhouse.com
Phone: 1-800-839-8640

Published by AuthorHouse 9/14/2012

ISBN: 978-1-4772-7024-0 (e)
ISBN: 978-1-4772-7025-7 (sc)

Library of Congress Control Number: 2012917356

Dare I share?

Dare I share with you all,

The darkness of this twisting hall,

A journey to the great within,

Scarier places you've never been,

Where chances of happy endings seem slim,

Where it's do or die, sink or swim,

Where nothing matters any more,

Except what is present at ones core,

And if that core be made of light,

You can always see a future bright,

For the light does shine from me to you,

Even if you don't wish it to,

Because in the end I'll see you there,

All our privacies stripped bare,

When all is gone you too will see,

Deep down you believe just like me.

So shall I strip first before you all here?

Show some of my most dark fears,

All my guilt and many sorrows,

Of all the yesterdays I wish back for tomorrows,

For now I see the error of my olds ways,

I wish back all those days,

When at a fork I did often pick,

That path that made my core so sick,

It's a long way back from those pits of despair,

To a place like heaven with out a care,

But travel that road I shall try,

Up until the day I die,

If any want to see my painful journey,

Just get me of this strapped up gurney,

Over to the computer and I will send thee,

A trip as ugly as can be,

But what once was ugly is no longer,

For it has only made me stronger,

To see this world I love so dear,

Drowning in a sea of tears,

With hell's fires raging around the globe,

Some one get the anal probe,

To see what makes us all so sick,

So much hate what makes us tick,

Well I believe I've had my fill,

Of all this misleading swill,

Those in power just keep it pouring,

I've long since found the charade quite boring,

So I've turned off all the news,

Only good for a case of the blues,

Ask and I shall try to take you to a place,

Where maybe you too can see his face.

Schizophrenia

Schizophrenia

Our modern lives have made us all,

Para"noids",

Rushing around until we fall,

As skits so frantic,

We've become manick,

Depressedants,

With delusions of grandeur,

And suicidal tendencies,

So next time your lives do race,

Your time here embrace,

For in the blink of his eye,

We all must die.

away we go

Mankind today is like lost sons,

Searching in the tempest night,

Lost but not forgotten,

By the only one who was begotten?,

For he calms the sea,

That they too may be,

At peace and rest in his father's arms,

Where none can do them any harm,

Even if their lives be given as tokens,

Their souls be saved by the truths he has spoken,

As they pledge their allegiance to his creed,

Man has become a better breed.

Spare any change?

a penny for your dying thoughts,

or feelings not yet you sought,

of you and I embraced as one,

not as children of a dying son,

but of children yet to be less sorrowed,

of a future we can build tomorrow,

of a love that we always will share,

by each person his god did fair,

make this dream of ours come true,

for he sowed it first so others might too.

a "common" man?

Who was this "crazy" man?

Teaching and healing throughout the land.

Claiming to be sent by God to deliver his word.

This task given to a simple commoner, how absurd.

Why didn't he select a king or a President?

Or at least a mansion's rich resident?

Words from these men can go a long way,

As we prove by obeying them each day.

Maybe send a lawyer, judge or magistrate?

For many men have they sealed their fate,

But they judge by a different book,

Not through the heart do they look,

Maybe send a doctor to heal our ills,

I'm sure they too wish it was as simple as pills,

He's sent rabbis, priests and cardinals apparently to look,

For their heads be buried too deep in their books,

Maybe send a teacher and such,

Would they concentrate on filling just the head too much?

Maybe send the soldier with all his might,

Maybe God didn't want to start another fight?

So did I forget any position in life?

Who could bring his word without all the strife?

Of judging each man by comparing one to another,

This can only serve to turn brother against brother,

For no one starts at the same spot,

From the time we are all just little tots,

Till we turn wrinkled, withered, and gray,

Only we can find our way,

To a better world of joy and peace,

No more pain, we've killed the beast,

But take if from one of this "crazy" guy's most loving fans,

God knew he had to send a "common" man.

For in the end we will see,

a common man like he,

shall save both you and me.

inposturme

oh, how you take my words,

be they mine yours or just for the birds,

for many a post i see, that tells of your love for me,

a child lost and seeking his father,

then almost saying why even bother,

for if the child be shabbily dressed,

give him clothes of permanent press,

so no wrinkle does his father see,

through all my faults it's still just me,

another wayward son,

just trying to have some fun,

despite all the sense of his rules,

we still all act the simple fools.

Jesus Still Saves On MLK

Jesus Still Saves On MLK?

This story that I'll try to rhyme,

Did truly happen to me one time.

It had been years since last in the saddle,

But how I could still make the suspension rattle.

Speeding down Broadway on my uptown boogey,

Dropped the window and hocked a loogey.

Back in the hood were I broke my "cherry",

The thrill and fear of those years still make me merry.

He was tired of the cube, even with a view,

Upon the carpet only his chair flew.

It was the contact of "real" people it seemed he missed,

Even if at times they did make him pissed.

Flying a box always in a race,

Cause after dark I didn't want my face.

To be in this hood where I felt hated,

I did my best not to be so jaded.

Too many was I just a honky without touching the horn,

So often the target of their scorn.

I tried my best to judge individually,

Could only hope they'd do the same for me.

So I found the only open spot,

Around here you take it illegal or not.

I did not return any of the hardened glares,

Brushed through the crowd concealing my cares.

At least to the best of my ability,

I often did this by faking tranquility.

Finally made contact with the store's keeper,

Jumping on the tailgate I dropped my beeper.

A pallet tipped to much and boxes flew to the ground,

It seemed more people were gathering round.

As if to see how whitey works,

My mishap just confirming we all must be jerks.

Finishing up I had the papers signed,

I had to move that truck or risk getting fined.

Shielded from traffic in front of the cab,

Waiting for it's break before the door could I grab.

Just around then I saw my second shadow appear,

One look in his eyes and I almost did fear.

You see I've been around and am not weak,

But compared to this guy my 230 frame seemed meek.

I think he could have played pro ball,

But was sure he could definately pro brawl.

I could see he had a P.H.D. from the school of hard knocks,

But yet I did not quake in my socks.

Knowing he wasn't standing in the street for his health,

I presumed he must be after my wealth.

So just before things seemed bout to go down,

I heard "Jesus saves, mother fuckers!" yelled and looked around.

One eye on the shadow and one searching for the preacher,

I thought of the words and ways of our teacher.

Then as a vision I saw them then,

Two men in blue that had just round the bend.

It was instantly apparent the "lunatic street preacher" that did shout,

Was nothing more then the perps look out.

So with a look like I'd just been saved

Was the perp's expression he had gave.

As my second shadow walked away,

I almost told him to have a nice day.

But just like that messiah long ago,

Those men in blue standing for justice did two sow.

Maybe it was wrong for me to presume?

That in these men's hearts for me was no room.

Either way, whether the "street preacher" knew or meant it not,

The truth was what he spoke on that spot.

Jesus loved us so much his life he had gave

So even this {M.F.keR?} his name could save.

I apologize to all for the profanity

But that's the way it happened that I did see.

fishpool parable

I was cleaning "my" brother's fish tank out after some weeks of neglect through all May's and June's showers I had no desire to deal with more dirty water till after the break in the weather. Well, after kicking up the covered walls with the magnascrubby, I proceeded to siphon filter the bottom and rock sediment. I drained the muddy water left to about half of 150 gallons give or take twenty. I filled to the top with hose water and was amazed after doing so at how cloudy and murky the "clear" water was still. (Don't look know but I think this is headed for another wanna those parallel parable thingamabobs) Then "my first son" Zachary an angel of five, whom happened to point out the muddied waters, asked if I could put a fish in the pool. I had long dreamt of the time when I could let the fishes into the pool and swim with them myself, so of course I obliged. I scooped but one I thought best up to the task. He wasn't the biggest or the boldest but a meek looking fellow of small stature but strong frame and conviction. I dropped him over the side and went to put on my trunks to swim with nature. lol. I "pampered" Zac and off we went to see our fish in action. He was swimming in the currents hiding off to the shade. I suppose to stay out of sight of predators. We swam and watched our little friend feel his freedom. I went for my glass of ice water and decided a good way to get the fish from pool to home tank. I chased him between my glass and the net. Hey swam into the glass not seeing its confines. It was a typical iced teas summer glass. I got a better look at it when I had him in. It had three distinct houses painted around its mid circumference. I watched him try to shoot through them in the clear spaces and bump head first into the invisible walls. I then began to see how this fish that actually was jumping and skipping out of the water to get away from and out of my net was now subdued by shadows on invisible walls. I lowered the glass and was dismayed to see the fish lower himself with it. The lip was at jumping level and he could easily jump it and be free to roam the huge heaven he had just found. But the 3 three big houses seem to be keeping him down below their ominous structures. They were all connected by a fence of some sort and that made it seem they were working together to keep him down. I lowered the lip a bit further and with some gentle coaxing and time he surfaced to freedom. Free from any burden the homes had put on him. I eventually recaptured him and put him back into his now clearer tank. I wonder what tales of fantasy he is telling his tank mates tonight about the heaven he once saw. Wonder if we'll ever see the water through the glass houses? p.s. I tested. The chlorine was nil and the ph was perfect. I hope I don't find a bunch of dried fish on my floor tomorrow. Never know if they get some crazy ideas of jumping the lip of their glass searching for a heaven ever last.

Poetic Amazonian Red Ant parable

Poetic parable of the red Amazonian ants

I wonder if many know of this crafty red species

That makes another black one clean up its feces

Bring them food and tend to their babies

They don't even let them have ladies

The reds don't work much except to give the orders

The blacks toil in the reds kingdom trapped in their borders

Never knowing they've been deceived

I wonder if they'd be relieved

To find out the truth of their plight

How when they were in the egg their was a fight

The reds took their army of mostly black drones

To raid another kingdom's thrones

The peaceful blacks did fight back

But I think the reds' venom do they lack

The black kingdom fell and their babies were taken

Only to be slaves the reds keep making

Maybe God wants us all

To keep learning how to make other kingdoms fall

But I think we've taught ourselves this quite well

For it does make our egos swell

To know our kingdom is the best

Because it gives no other kingdoms rest

To keep up their defenses they must

No other kingdom can they trust

I wonder if God's gavel fell

Would all those reds ants go to hell?

Well read!

Woeezme,

I suppose to much tv,

Should read a book instead,

Better off to fill my head,

With words and phrases,

That get great praises,

From those that delight,

In flexing their might,

With pen or with sword,

The never get bored,

Of driving home their point,

That they run this joint,

So do what you must,

Go on and kick up a fuss,

For it will do you no good,

Like you desire it would,

For what knowledge they have in their heads,

Does make them well, reds.

Booty parabel

Dearest flumc, you still with us, if only occasionally? I found another parallel I'll try to make into a parable for you, if it helps to please me or pleases to help you. I'm a father, not presently worthy of the title, but will use it for parable purposes only. Lil George sleeps soundly down the hall snug in the realative safety and comfort I can some how manage to still supply. Be it begged, borrowed or stolen from one of my many "brothers". Every morning I hear him begin to rustle. He wakes happy for the most part, knowing all is well and the day is new and good as far as now as he knows it. Some how, this boy genius of 8 months, has already figure out the the communication device at the foot of his crib get's him in touch with his father, the source of all his salvation. For the father feeds, cloths,cleans and teaches him, both body and soul. So in his quest to get to the device of salvation he begins to struggle, twisting and turning not always sure his direction is true. He hears the garbled static and knows if he can only reach the device his cries for help will be answered. I listen with some amazement at his resolve and determination. Then as I hear his breathing grow louder and know he has the device in sights. He still crawls "backward" so he ingeniusly pulls the sheets the device lays on. Finally I hear him nawing on the device and making indistinguishable pleas for help in baby talk, of course. His frustration mounts for his calls seem to go unanswered. He sees not my foot hit the floor and me stirring from my bed to come to his aid. In his impatience and frustration he pulls too hard on the device and the cord unplugs. I hear the static of a lost connection and he hears the silence of what he must think is me abandoning him. He begins to cry more and more in earnest as I make my way down the hall. I find him sprawled in all directions, the device still in his grasp, crying. I stand at a distance slightly calling him. He stops crying to lend his ear. He looks to find me upside down in his eyes now. It takes but a fix into my eyes and our inverted frowns are neither up nor down, for they are smiles not frowns at all. He knows his device wasn't were his salvation was but in the heart and soul of his father and therefore in himself for he was made in the image of his father. But now my image has been cracked for I've lost my way and look for my device to call to my father. But it's on a human scale. The device could be a book but that is not where our salvation lies, it lies within the image and spirit of all our fathers.

Help me bring the spirit of god back to all mankind for all your books

have failed us myserably for i see not many smiles but tears in our

unions today. Peace and sorry if my parallel isn't a better parable.

I See and Am Sure

It's first through a roar,

That I hear it's allure.

Then through smell,

That I can tell.

By the first salty taste,

The warmth of the sun upon my face.

It's in the touch of a toe,

That I know.

Upon a gentle summer's breeze,

All my troubles begin to ease.

Once I sea,

Then I am shore.

It's my love of the beach,

I do preach.

For when I am there,

I have no care.

When like a grain of sand am I,

My spirit does fly.

The Ain't I Christ?

So what if you too came with "your version" of his word?

From your God or soul you claim to have heard.

And of your own doubts that you can live it,

Are you worthy enough that you should try to give it?

To another who might make of it more then you?

Who may actually be able to keep it true?

Who may receive it with total grace?

To make this world a more heavenly place.

Would they not see it through all your flaws?

Of how you're not able to live perfectly by his laws?

Your constant battle with demons that you do fight.

Should you feel the wrath of all their or just his might?

Even though you mean no one harm,

Does his word lose its charm?

Would they see through all your weakness?

And if so, would you lose all your meekness?

If you screamed from the top of your voice,

That we all must soon make a choice.

To either admit defeat and die in vain,

Or make our souls journey to another plain.

And if one such as you and I stood,

Would it do us any good?

For those in power don't believe it so

That it's the only way we must go.

To keep our species always advancing,

Is any willing to keep on chancing?

That those which we've mistakenly put up too high,

Won't make it all our reason to die.

For when we take our and his power from them,

Would we wake these thieves from their dens?

Would they put us all through hell?

Because we believe in the one that fell,

Under their judgment and how they did "kill" him.

So that they might have their every whim.

But what they might all fail to admit,

Is that they are all just captains of their sinking ships.

For he has shown them the only way to navigate,

The only way through heaven's strait.

For his beacon will forever be lit,

So any good captain's boat might fit.

Through the danger we all must see,

That it's time for a mutiny?

I see it's time to pick up our crosses,

It's the only way to minimize our losses.

And if this sinners words could make your world fall,

Is your world worthy to stand at all?

Call in the Calvary

I'm sure this is neither the time nor place for most of you to see this here, but it is Christmas so I'm letting it go. Again. It's not a pretty poem so if you don't finish it I understand. Most of you will not like it. Many will hate me for it. Think I put myself too high. Probably right, but we gotta try. It's horribly written, but it was done through the nashing of teeth so you all might not have too. lol I hope somebody likes it. I know it's many different things to so many. here it is. I dare.

Man's confession to God

Or just

The Ramblings of a Madman?

Hello to all,

I know you're probably all mad that I sent this to everybody, but lend me your ear and I will try to make it worth your while. Since I probably will get fired for breaking the cardinal rule of stopping the production line we call progress, please read this in its entirety. For the message to truly begotten it must be read as it was written. EXTREMELY

PAINFULLY, BUT DUTIFULLY AND DILIGENTLY. If you can muster the strength and courage to look at these things you will be greatly rewarded. Really try to put yourself in the writer's place. Hopefully you, like I, will be totally amazed at what this can do for you. If it makes you think or better yet "feel", then act. Send it on too as many people around the world as you possibly can. Please don't alter its contents in anyway except for possibly spelling. Don't jeopardize your jobs, unless of course you feel after reading this that getting this message out is more important then any one of us or at least our jobs. Translate it in as many languages as you can and send it over the web. Use the web for more than busines$ and pornography for a change. I have been asking myself a few questions and would like to share them with you all. Is it a total sell out? Has each and every one of us sold his soul to the devil for a new bigger SUV or a 6,000 square foot house? Because if we did, I don't think I got my money's worth. DO YOU? Do any of us care what's happening in or to today's world? Do you care what's happening to any one besides yourself or only if it's in our nations "vital" interest$? Which translates "what or how much is in it for us"? Are we all so self absorbed worrying about what next over indulgent toy we can buy for ourselves or how our stocks did today that we don't care that the new bigger pollution device you're buying is destroying your children's environment and therefore their health and futures? Do we care that the extra hundreds of trees you took down to build that extravagant home for all three of you also helps to fuel this problem? Or the companies you're investing in sells kiddy porn or enslave children into working, saves millions by illegally dumping nuclear waste or sells weapons to terrorist groups. What about all the less fortunate in the world who don't have a coat to pull over their heads in a storm? What about our glutinous ways of eating? We are over indulging in this respect as well. We throw out as much, if not more, food as we consume and still hold onto food we can't eat, so not to give it away to the starving and ruin our economy? To hell with them, right? Let them work for theirs too. People are constantly saying money is the root to all evil. I'm inclined to believe these people. Where are all the smart and righteous engineers and scientists getting rich off the ideas on how to stop this love affair with the deadly polluting gas combustion engine? We know or hear they have engines that produce water as an exhaust or run on water but for some reason they won't use them. No money in it!!?? That can't be so. Wouldn't you like to buy a device that will help insure the quality of life for you children as well as their children? Where are all the great philosophers or our children's' teachers for that matter getting rich spreading higher idea of our inner being and of our drive to learn? Or where are the ones getting rich on a way to get rid of all these weapons of mass destruction, nuclear and chemical devices, by making them obsolete? Where are the "good" politicians and/or lawyers not worrying about how much money the can make in kick backs, pay offs and other forms or bribery but doing good for the people's sake not for their own? That's their intended role but they sold us out. Maybe these sinners are the ones who separated church and state so they can do whatever evil suits them. Because they are not religious they will not allow us to be in our society. Where are all the people getting rich on selling or making movies and books about the good we all posses within ourselves? Instead, we go to see Hannibal on Saint Valentine's Day. We go home and watch wrestling, Gerry Springer, Dark Angel or some other less obviously demoralizing and life demeaning shows as the Simpsons, Friends and Sex in the City etc... Starting to sound a bit like Sodom & Gomorra. Even the history channel and TLC only put on the history of wars and serial killers and the secret societies that our running the governments of the world today. What do most of these government officials have in common anyway. Their love of money and power. Not their love of humanity. Have they done good for the people of the world as a whole or just for the few million that live in their rich or poor countries? Have they done any real good for their own countries at all? Is all the news in the world bad? Has nothing good happened in the last few years? Is their any good left in the world? Or have we sold all of that too? Or are we all too busy trying to get what's coming to us, to stop to look for the good in us all? To demand it! To make it! Or better yet to be it!! If we are not diligent in looking for as well as creating this good, we will all get what's coming to us. I know all the negative shit sells. But I know that good sells too (it's a Wonderful life, "oh God" etc.) Is it a coincidence that we are seeing these types of life affirming and soul searching films less and less? Can you believe I can't think of any others with all the negative shit pumped into my head daily? Can you? Nobody's selling the good stuff!! So stop buying into all of this negative and harmful stuff. Turn off your sets. Stop watching life as they want you to see it and start living it as you should be living it. This TV time is a quick and useless way of self gratification watching others either do what you should never do or probably be doing yourself. If you had the time and still had the money to do them. Again it goes back to time/ money. If time is money why didn't we use time for money? Because the greedy can't horde time. Therefore giving us a test of our own goodness and giving evil a way into our society from the top down. Help yourselves by helping others. God helps those that help themselves. Work so many hours at a job and everybody gets a "fair" allowance for this time. Something like this could be devised if we followed the golden rule and stopped trying to take what our brother has. As it is now see where the real money goes. Lawyers getting murderers and politicians off. Multi-million dollar bonuses to CEOs who lay off thousands of people for what's best for the share holders not what's best for the people as a whole. If 5 or 10 % of the people in this world have 95% of the wealth in the entire world then wouldn't they also own 95% of all major companies? Therefore only doing what's best for themselves as the major shareholders. Does this make sense to you? Is this a sustainable society? No, it's not. All of those harmful movies and other forms of "entertainment" your paying to see. Shouldn't some of these billions go to other more worth while things instead? Our brothers would give us what we needed and we them if we all just followed the rules. Then we could seek jobs we liked and everyone would be happier. We could figure out a way to make these computers and robots be our slaves instead of us slaves to them. We could be free to pursue some real worth while goals like self enlightenment, helping others and maybe we could even find out what the true meaning of our existence is etc… There is so much more we could be doing with what we have. Don't we all see that? Is that the test we are all taking? We must figure out that we've been dropped onto this world by our "father", make him what you like, spirit, alien, simian, what ever. Most of you are parents. What would you say to your children if you had to leave them alone to fend for themselves? You'd tell them not to fight with each other, don't steal each others stuff, share and play nicely, clean up after yourselves and take care of your "pets" for they are beings that may not be as smart as you but they are still my creations. ESPECIALLY IF YOUR CHILDREN HAD THE "SMARTS" TO KILL ALL OF THEMSELVES!!! What have we done? We've turned our backs on all these simple rules. We've taken from the weaker ones of the world and conquered our brothers. We've made quite a mess of the place doing so too. We've exploited God's many creatures and have totally eliminated hundreds of species entirely and are still doing so today. If we all got together under one belief that these ten basic laws or just the golden rule should not be violated or broken in our society. We should strive to really help those that break these commandments, (if we the decent majority would help the less fortunate, as we should be doing, you would be shocked by the drop in crime because there would be less "have knots" trying to get theirs/yours da.) And not by locking them up and throwing away the key, but by showing them the error of their ways by being examples of our good ways. Who decided that both parents had to work to live "comfortably" anyway? We did. That's who. Comfortably used to mean a roof over your head and food in your belly. Now it's a vacation home at the beach, (if we obeyed the rules we all could have these things and much more) a new car for everybody and a boat and a motorcycle and etc... While the 5 or 10 percent of the richest "elite" don't work at all and are getting richer off our backs. These people can say what they want, to themselves as well as their judge on judgment day, but nobody believes the billions of dollars they horde grow on trees. They grow in some poor exploited countries oil fields. They grow in mines of other poor starving countries. They grow in dark basement sweat shops that make your nice cloths so affordable. They grow on our backs too. The "good" simple folk of the working class people of the world. If time is money, by racing to grab as much as possible, aren't you really taking some body's time here on earth? THINK ABOUT THAT. Sure some of these countries are poor, but they have the richest "elite" in the world. We watch them go by in their Lexus and Mercedes and wish we were like them. Had what they had. So we sell them more of our time or sell each other out to make more money and the cycle continues. Until all we have left is a big house, a nice car, a broken family (divorce is inevitable today) we barely recognize and that has been turned into something we don't want to see. Because we weren't there to raise them right. Or have we forgotten what is right? So we now pay other people to raise our children for us when we should be sacrificing our time and money because we want to spend time with them. Some of these people are only in it for the money too. So they really don't care about your children as much as you, the parents are supposed to. And the love these children miss is painfully obvious. It manifests itself in all forms of horrible things these children some as young as 5 are doing to each other. If it's not sex, it's violence. I wonder where they get it all from? Sex and violence is all people want, right? I refuse to believe this. We must be here for some thing better than this. Most of us should agree that a higher, smarter and or more compassionate being/s (let's hope they don't possess the evil we've shown too each other) have visited earth in the past. We are still trying to figure out how "primitive" people built things 4000 years ago that we cannot build today using "modern" technology. Isn't it ironic that we have these symbols of the faros greed and domination of their fellow man pasted on the almighty U.S. dollar? These poor people who built these pyramids weren't slaves? They were rats racing after as much cheese as they could get for themselves as the ship they were on was sinking. Sound familiar!!! Whether it was Mohammed, Jesus, or aliens for that matter we can not be positive or agree completely on. But one thing most of us can agree on is that some one pretty smart gave us some very simple rules to live by. They even told us that if we did not live by these rules then we would surely die by them. I think they are still called the 10 commandments but I'm not sure if there is a copy right law on this phrase pending litigation$. BUT I'D MAKE A BET THERE IS!!! I believe these commandments are the only way we can every create heaven here on Earth. Or we can survive on Earth for that matter. Or survive long enough to figure out how to fly back to heaven or to fly out and create a new one. Maybe we (aliens) ran out of fuel or time on the space ship or just liked earth's possibilities. Maybe this (earth) is the only heaven we as a being could ever get to. Maybe we all have to get there together or none of us can go? Maybe when we all bring our souls and inner being together toward the same goal, like many insects in the world do, we would create Eden as it was meant to be. What is it that is really telling all of these "FEEBLE MINDED" insects to work together for the better good of the whole? IS IT EVOLUTION? THINK ABOUT THAT. Will we destroy ourselves or each other before we can evolve into better "beings"? Are we never to see Eden again? Why not? Most religions teach us to save as many people's souls as you possibly can. The more the merrier sort of thing. We are also taught through many or most religions that God loves all of us. Why can't we love each other as he loves us all, regardless of our differences? Weren't we made in his image? If he can do it shouldn't we be able to? He told us we could, didn't he. Maybe we will get it right the next time around. Maybe this is the last time around. Maybe we can change the ending to the book. Maybe somebody rewrote the ending of the book. What greater power would be so spiteful as to tell us the ending to this great journey we are all on? Think about that. Maybe we have lost a lot of the battles but can still win the war. Here and now. Where are all the good guys? I'm not talking about the soldiers killing the mad religious nuts out there trying to save the world from our evil ways. Are these groups really nuts anyway? IF THEY PROMOTE KILLING OTHERS FOR EVIL THEY ARE. YOU CAN BE SURE OF THAT. AND IF YOU GET THIS MESSAGE YOU CAN CERTAINLY IDENTIFY THESE GROUPS. Because they can no longer hide their ways from you. You have the knowledge to see all as it truly is. I love this country and for what we believe it stands for, at least stood for. But lately I've not seen much good come from it. DO WE REALLY WANT TO BE THE "LEADERS" OF THE WORLD THAT IS ONLY DESTINED TO END IN TOTAL ANNIHILLATION AND DESTRUCTION? Do we really want to defend or propagate a society that puts money above all else and sells our children's' futures out? Do we really do want to defend our "freedom of speech", where we are free to say, sing and show any despicable act and lewd behavior in the guise of entertainment, THINGS WE SHOULDN'T BE ENDORSING, but we are not allowed to say a prayer in our schools, THINGS WE SHOULD BE PROMOTING? DOES THIS MAKE SENSE TO YOU? I believe the majority of all peoples are good hearted souls. Either "informed" or not. I'd estimate that the ratio is probably around 70/30 in favor of the good people. Shine your "light" on them. Does the majority still reflect it back? Or better yet do they show you their "light" and maybe it's brighter than your own. Don't we all see that by sharing and showing this "light" with each other we gain the strength of it with in us all!! Don't we see that, yet? Or do we need another world war to show our good sides as a whole? Do we have to learn this lesson the hard way for at least the third time? Da. Haven't we learned this lesson already? And it will be contagious as evil ways are. But with this continuous bombardment of evil propagating techniques presently employed by our societies, here and abroad, I believe the ration of good/bad hearted people is sliding at an alarming rate. I believe further more that once this ratio is at an unreasonable or unacceptable ratio we will kill our world. IF YOU WERE OUT NUMBERED BY MORE THAN 2 TO 1

WHAT WOULD YOU DO? MAYBE YOU WOULD SPLIT THEIR FORCES AND ATTACK THEM FROM WITHIN? SOUND FAMILIAR? Is this what's happened to us all? Better yet, can we do it to "them" among us all? Did we split into separate countries or were we pulled apart by "them" these evil money tycoons staking their claims in this world. By keeping us good hearted souls divided by nation, race, religion(same basic rules for all just a "slightly" different spin put on each), age, sex, sexual orientation, and or social/economic status and yes even by political party, they are winning this war of evil. If we could send the message of the true meaning of these commandments, by starting to live by them, to each and everyone in the world, maybe we can begin to turn this evil and decadent spiral around. After all, we are the "leaders" of the "free" world. Or are we merely sheep led to the slaughter? Our shepherd has given us the 10 tools to protect ourselves from the evil madness. I say we start using them. Maybe we could take our couple of hundred dollar tax break, it's in the tens/hundred thousands for the elite, (maybe the elite rich are trying to appease you from taking action against them!?)We could send it or even just some of it to the starving masses and homeless of the world here and abroad. If of course we could ensure that the greedy didn't steal it in the process,(Somalia) as a jester of our country's peoples' true commitment to doing the right thing by everyone in the world not just ourselves? Even if we can't buy a new Jacuzzi this year. Share, share it's only fair. Is something I say to my nieces and nephews on a daily basis? Are we the people of the "best" or at least the "strongest" country in this sick and depraved world really sharing the wealth of the world with the masses? No, is the answer. Are we even sharing the wealth with ourselves? No, is the answer. Start to think, feel and do something about these things. What would you really do for money? What are you really doing for your money? What are you making others do or become for your money? Who are you taking it and or time from? I still have to figure that out for myself. Don't be so foolish as to think "your" money grew on some tree and you didn't hurt anybody by getting it. Did your company? Should you be working for a company that's done some of the most despicable acts, in the name of progress and money, to your fellow man? I know. What can I do? I'm just one person. BULLSHIT. The men/them with their fingers on the buttons are only one person too. Are we going to sit back and watch what devastation and destruction these men can create? I know, it's destiny right? Well if that's so, then why aren't more of us living more righteous lives? I know. Only so many are to be saved, right? And we all pray and think that it's our religion, right? I'm not a very religious person, or at least I wasn't, until I started to ponder the errors of my/our ways. Some serious forces are at work here, good and evil with in us all, and we must take a stand and fight back against the evil in this world. Abroad and ESPECIALLY HERE AT HOME. FOR THIS IS "OUR" HOME!!! DON'T LET THEM DIVIDE US THE GOOD AND RIGHTEOUS MAJORITY!!!! Sure we can't agree on everything, but if we agreed on living by these 10 commandments we wouldn't go to war over one single dispute. Including and especially this so call HOLY WAR!!!! Let he who is without sin and truly pure of soul claim the holiest land of all our major religions his rightful place of ownership or better yet his (selfish) home. If they both are killing for this sacred land then what does that say about these peoples' souls?? You know the answer. Two wrongs do not make a right! All these people should be aloud to weep together at the wall in shame for their sins against all mankind. These sinners killing each other and innocent others, over this land must be out of their minds and definitely out of touch with their souls if they believe God, even a vengeful god, would put ANY land before men's lives and souls. It's not the land, or where these messages of true enlightenment happened to take place, (it takes place with in your soul) at a time when our world was ruled again by the greedy money changers, but of the message that was bestowed upon us. HEAR THIS

MESSAGE A NEW!!! Don't kill in the name of the lord but only in defense of "ourselves". Whomever your lord happens to be, or for land or oil or money etc... CALLING ALL GOOD PEOPLE!! WAKE UP!!! The world maybe coming to an end and this isn't some movie where we can change the channel. That's right. It really comes down to good against evil. EITHER YOU'RE FOR THE GOOD OF THE WHOLE OF MANKIND, DOWN TO THE LAST, OR YOU'RE NO GOOD AT ALL!!! DON'T WE UNDERSTAND THAT, YET? We must get together and show ourselves. If you're not ready to truly receive this message then just keep trying. Have faith in yourself and your brothers. Demonstrate against these wicked things. Call them what you like but the way they are used is wicked. Boycott products such as movies and games that promote these things. ESPECIALLY IF THEY ARE DIRECTED AT OUR CHILDREN!! Get together and be heard. Be seen. Care. Get involved. Who are they? We, the not yet "informed" are they. Maybe aliens are they. Maybe the devil and his followers are they. Trying to make us end the world so they can take it over or keep control of it? DON'T YOU SEE THAT "LOGIC"? IT'S ONLY "COMMON" SENSE! Something to think about, isn't it? If they were smart enough to get here they have to be smarter than us? We must out number them or are just their servants. Think about it. We shouldn't worry so much about exposing "them" but showing ourselves as we truly want to be. If that's fighting, stealing, cheating, lying, killing etc... We've seen enough of you already. STAY HOME!! I'm talking about the people who want changes to happen in a positive way. We can only have true strength if we bond together as a new world church of some sort, or get all the nations and religions to agree on these sacred ideas (if they don't already), following the ten commandments or the golden rule with out all the different spins on how we got them and who's going to be saved and who should be killed in the name of our nation or religion. These negative spins can only be "their" words any way, right?! I know "new world order". I was scared of that too. But if we have a new world church based on the commandments and the masses INCLUDING AND ESPECIALLY those in power obey these rules, how can that be bad?! If we make a stand and the elite cause a distraction, nuclear or chemical terrorists war/etc... Will you see it as the end or as a diversion to keep us split up??!! WAKE UP!! WE HAVEN'T MUCH TIME!! We've already proven we can conquer one another. Let's prove we can conquer ourselves by doing the right thing by one another. If we are all destined to go out in a ball of destruction, fire and brimstone, let's go out with some dignity, honor, morals, love and compassion. No, I'm not gay because I love my fellow man, woman and child. IF THAT REALLY MATTERS TO YOU!! Why does everybody want to be the bad guy today? It's o.k. to be the good guy. Let's fight the good fight. Don't go quietly into the night but rage against the darkness. Don't endorse and fund this perpetual slide into depravity in its many forms. It's up to each of us to seek out this evil and to get rid of it. At least get rid of it from our lives and lead our children by example; by taking care of their futures. In the most peaceful manner possible. Just don't join the frenzy. Don't watch, listen or buy any off the products that promote violence or death toward one another, raping or pornography and other sexual deviant acts for that matter. This includes us so called grown ups who have seen enough of this stuff to last us an eternity (maybe this will be your eternity!!) yet we still watch it to see if we can be shocked by how depraved and indifferent we people can be to each other. GROW UP!!! EVOLVE ALREADY!! We are all acting like spoiled and rotten children and our "father" is going to punish us for it. Demand that they produce the cleanest engines (not gas/oil powered)!! We know the have the technology to make better cleaner burning engines and have had for some time. But we can't get the oil moguls and or our selfish selves for that matter moving into a cleaner more environmentally sound practices fast enough for our environmental safety concerns with out them giving up their money/political power or us sacrificing our own need for speed(selfish). Get in the streets and protest. Don't drive to work for a week, a month. DO SOMETHING TOGETHER AS A PROTEST OF YOUR FRUSTRATIONS OF THE WORLD TODAY. This is just one of the power aspects you receive with this message. Maybe, if we joined together and stopped this money machine long enough, we could change things for the better. See if they hear our voices. See if they listen. If they want your money show them you want some real "goods" or good services for them. Not this garbage they have been feeding us. Help some one with your money, don't hurt children with it. Stop the violent cartoon watching and play with your kids. You'd be surprised at the spiritual as well as physical lift you will get trying to keep up with them. Can't you see the spiritual innocence in their eyes??! Don't we all want that feeling of innocence back?? I KNOW I DO!!!!. Don't allow them to watch bad natured "adult" programming while you're at the bar or hotel room cheating on your spouse. How can we look in our children's eyes and the go out into the world and ruin their lives? Don't we all get it?? By saving the children we save ourselves. Don't let your children buy these products either. No matter how hard they beg. Explain to them that although it may be cool with those other kids, but it goes against your moral beliefs and could seriously damage their spiritual health. There is such a thing you know?? As a small boy, have you ever helped an old lady by shoveling her driveway for her? Fully expecting to get paid, of course. And when she goes to give you the money you refuse it knowing she probably needs it more being alone and on a tight budget. Or any small or insignificant gesture to some one on the phone or in your car or where ever. Don't we all see that the little gestures of kindness can mean the most? But, do you know who they mean the most to? Is it you or the lady? Maybe it's to the almighty himself. It's your way of affirming your commitment to his ways. Of you not saying, I'm just one insignificant individual. What can I do? That cop out must be the most used phrase he hears or we use for that matter. Have you felt that small but great feeling of achievement? Like you just took one more step toward a great and mighty goal. Well, I believe you have. We must all begin to take these steps in our every day lives and do so in a hurry. Run, don't walk!! I have committed many sins in my time and have been striving on working them out. To make amends for them. So, I say these things sitting here crying for them and for all the other sins I've let pass before my eyes and did nothing to stop or even deter them. I'm scared. Aren't you? I'm scared for myself. I'm scared for the children and what they will have to endure should we fail in our mission. I fear it may be too little too late. I can only hope it's not too late for me to save my soul. IT'S NOT TOO LATE FOR US ALL TO SAVE THE CHILDREN FROM THE FATE WE ARE BESTOWING UPON THEM. I'm scared because I've never seen these things I've seen in the last few days. What if some of these things coming to me are right? What if the answer comes to you? Will you see it? Don't you see it? Don't we all see it? If you can't see it with your minds then see it with your hearts and souls. What happens after we all truly see the truth? Does a great white light flash and take us to the great beyond. I certainly hope so. Because I can see the future we are presently bound for and it's not a pretty sight. Faith is hope. We must always hold on to our hope and faith even and especially in this time of great turmoil to come. I'm going to start to try. How hard can it be to follow ten common sense rules? Ha, ha. Maybe it's not too late for you too. For those of you who are selling out your fellow man, woman or child for the almighty dollar, maybe it's not too late for you either. Don't sell that uranium to those terrorists. Don't be a spy selling us out. Don't exploit peoples sad and depraved lives by showing them on TV and watch them fighting each other. Don't watch these shows either (all of today's talk shows are doing it) go seek out these troubled people and help them find their ways. To come with us. REALLY HELP THEM. Check out the clothes you buy, the cheaper they are the more they usually cost someone else (not money wise of course) Think about that and you will see its truth. Produce that engine that helps the environment no matter how much they pay you to bury it some where. What the hell, do it for practically nothing. Or better yet do it for everyone. That only depends on how you really look at it. Make a descent movie that promotes the good with in us all. If it doesn't make you rich at least it isn't hurting anybody and everybody by endorsing these sins and showing them to our as well as "his" children. What are all you people going to do with the money after the world is over anyway? Can it save you from the end? Will it save your children? Can you buy your way out of hell with it? What is wrong with all these people sitting on millions upon millions of dollars? You and I know who some of them are. Don't they have souls? Don't they know that by amassing these great fortunes they've won the game played on this world but have lost the purpose and meaning of what this world was supposed to be about. LOVE. For one another, for ourselves, for our children and the animals and Mother Nature etc... Yeah, I used the four letter word. It's not so bad. Try it. Have you grown up enough to tell your father that you love him? Or that's not manly. If possessing and expressing the greatest thing a person can display on this planet is not manly then none of us are worthy of receiving it. And that's exactly why our marriages are failing and our children our killing parents and other etc... Spend more time with your children. Tell them what you believe is right and what you think is morally wrong. If the world should end for the majority of us, they are our only hope for the next run at heaven here on earth. We and the lord must try to ensure that the remaining people are of the same sort of beliefs. But they must believe them stronger then we have. Did you ever notice that the two things you should never talk about, religion and politics are the two most important subjects in our lives? One is how we think we should live our lives and the other is how "our" leaders actually allow or enable us to live them by promoting any and all ideas and way of life they want. Sometimes regardless of what's best for US? If we don't talk about politics how do we know what each other believes? Would you know propaganda if you saw it on your TV? Aren't we tired of seeing the same old war, sex and violence on our TVs? Terrestrial vision. Maybe the evil, the aliens or the greedy are sealing their fate by completing their deal with the devil? They sell us the evil and see how many of us bite. Have we all taken the bait? Then we think it's o.k. to do what we see. SHUT THEM OFF AND SEE THE TRUE LIGHT. Did we go to the moon? Was there an election or did these guys bid on the presidency right up to the last minute? Is big brother or the forces behind the money going to kill me or worse for saying all of this? He's probably going to fire me, that's for sure. And I can easily live with that. If in this fight they may take up against me for my/our/his words brings harm to my loved ones then I truly am sorry and will be heart broken. Unless of course I give them this message first. But I believe this message is more important then my family or any body's family or country or race or etc... I hope you get this message too. If it helps just one of you live a better life. And if he or some on else does silence me, will you continue to fight and save your soul/society/mankind and as many others as you possibly can? Regardless if you think you can achieve this goal? Are you worthy of being saved? Are your children? Am I? If you noticed, I use "we" and "maybe" a lot in this confession of ours. This is to show my involvement in these moral shortcomings and to admit that my faith is not your faith. Maybe you believe in the higher alien power. Is that another name God goes by? We all know he has many names and some believe no name is worthy of him. I use "him" because I'm a male and therefore I was created in his name. You can use what you like. I think we get the idea. I've been and still am guilty of a lot of these bad things around us all. Mostly of sitting idly by as these horrible things come to be. I can only hope and keep trying to be worthy of salvation when it's my turn to meet my maker and hopefully spread the word. That we are good. We want and need to be good. If we don't, we will lose all that is good. May god save us all. And if you don't believe in god, maybe it's a real good time to start to. These are just some of the thoughts I've been having. What do you think is going on? All of these ideas rushed into my head in a short few days. They may not all be correct but I think I've gotten the general idea of what this life is for. It's for us. It's his gift to us. It's his test of us. Can't we see that? We can make it happen. We can make it heaven. WE'VE GOT TO MAKE IT HAPPEN! Talk about it. Do something about it. Before it's too late. Is that mankind's AKA humanity's epitaph going to read "they all saw it coming the whole time, but they just sat back and watched it happen!" I know it's hard in these troubling times but have faith enough to hope and try to change these things. For if we don't try we've already lost the war.

p.s. I don't know why all of a sudden my thoughts have come to these realization. Maybe it's the fact that we all see it coming and live with this feeling of doom on a daily basis. I know I've just scratched the surface of some very difficult and touchy subjects and am probably wrong on some. But you must admit. We have and are letting ourselves go morally as the leaders of the "free" world. Don't even get me started on the politicians, lawyers and the big money moguls that control them. I'd imagine politics is the biggest industry in the world second only to the Churches. That's probably true in just the money we see on the books not to mention the billions of lobbyists dollars and backing from the rich and powerful as well as each and every one of us making our contributions to the pot. In today's world, with the internet and other computing devices why do we need these people making our decisions for us anyway? Why not have a vote on most of the issues and let the "moral" majority rule? Because the money moguls can't buy us all out. THAT'S WHY! The money pulls these greedy sinners strings, both politicians and the churches, into making the worst possible decisions for the greatest good of mankind. I strike out at the churches for we all know they have more money then god and do relatively little good, at least that I can see, with it. Would god really want a Vatican city or some glorious Mosk or Temple or would he want you to take that money and give it to the needy people of the world? The televangelists duping the sick and stupid into giving them billions for their own mansions not the starving and sick masses the money was intended to help. Maybe this is a timed test and time is almost up. These rich and powerful elite fighting over the riches of the world will be the end of it all. Bin laden is a billionaire too. If we allow them and ourselves to continue this sick and deprave race for as much cheese as we rats can get our hands on while the ship we are all on is sinking we will destroy ourselves. Because we've sold them our intelligence and souls by giving them the power to destroy our world while they fight for its riches. I'm ashamed it's taken me this many years to realize or even stop to think about what's really going on. I know this sounds crazy and I will probably doom myself for saying this but it's as if someone has showed me all of this instantly. And the truly sad part is that it's been right under my/our noses the whole time. The most obvious things can be the hardest to see. Maybe that's why they say to be ware of false prophets. These false prophets are us not yet informed. Maybe if we were all true prophets of his beliefs we would win the war against the evil within ourselves. Am I a false prophet? I hope not. I want to be a follower of the rules not the ruler of men. I hope you can all see the truth in my words. I hope all of you become the true prophets of his rules. How long must they kill our prophets while we stand around and watch any way? Sound familiar? IT'S TRUE!! Why would you let them silence this word of religion and free speech anyway? Isn't that what this country was founded on anyway? Or were we merely tired of giving some foreign country our money? This is the gold we should all be racing after. By freeing our souls we could stop living in these gilded cages we've built for ourselves. Are any of us rats in this race we call progress truly as happy as we can be? Do you se your fellow workers smiling and saying the littlest gestures like hi or how are you? Do we still even care about these people or are they just our competition in this rat race? So they should be taken out one way or the other so you can beat them and take their share of the money in this world. I must have really been busy indulging myself and preoccupying my time with what I've got coming to me. Maybe I've finally lost my mind in this crazy world. Maybe I've just begun to find my soul and or conscious. Have you talked to yours lately? Maybe I'm more worried about where my soul is going to reside in the after life, or if we don't have souls maybe I'm more worried about what the children of the world will go through or miss. I worry about these things more now than which country I'm from on this small planet or how big my house, car is etc... I apologize to any one I've insulted or have waist their time reading this and to my company I work for. These ideas are mine (?) and do not represent ATT in any way. Unless of course they (ATT) want to sign on to some of these ideas. Which it can't because it would get sued by some no religious/ethical group saying that the companies and government we work and live in can't show their religious or moral beliefs or what have you. We the people don't want any large monetary or governmental institutions getting involved in religions moral beliefs. OR DO WE? But I'm sure if this were suddenly to become financially beneficial to these institutions and people they would make an exception to the rule. I'm sure if our government officials and those of all countries followed these golden rules the world would not be such a mess. Remember there are more of us good then them, at least for now. You the richest of the world, search for your souls if you can still find them beneath all that money, and see if what I'm saying strikes a chord. I hope you too will be saved. By saving others I believe you can save yourselves. You must believe you can too. Some of you that we have made so rich can buys and sell entire countries. Yet you sit back and watch as children of god starve to death. You are truly sick from within and I believe I've found a cure for you. Find it for yourselves. Look at your souls and tell me if the message isn't emblazoned on it. If you had all that money would you sit on it and buy more material things then you could ever use or need with out helping others? Are we all sitting on it? I hope not. Maybe we all have too much already. I mean really helping others. Not by giving them unessential things but by giving them food and shelter. Some of these people give generously to charity but the truth is they only do it so not to give the government more. Real morality for you isn't it? But there are millions doing the same and worse. Does anybody remember when this country had some crazy movement none as the HIPPIES? That was based on a principal of peace and love toward all mankind, if my memory server me correctly, and a few other unmentionables. But could you imagine if we cleaned up some of the undesirable traits they had endorsed and replaced them with the real message? We would still have a peaceful and loving society uplifted by the enlightenment and knowledge we would gain if we truly realized why we are here? Instead we took the decadent things like over sex and drugs and the money that goes with them and dropped the peace and love and replaced it with things like war, crime and hate. OH MY GOD!!! I'm in hell aren't I? Aren't you yet? If you receive this message then act on it. It is the only way!! It's so very obvious so don't let the others not yet enlightened pull you down or lead you into being fooled. They are our responsibility too. If we don't help those that need us most we are all guilty of sin. Please god, I'm no longer afraid come and get me!! Could you imagine if we gave the truly divine people, some sort of alien beings with in us all, the power of our world as one? OH MY GOD!!! WHAT ARE YOU TELLING ME?? PLEASE STOP SHOWING ME THIS. Am I going mad or have I found the answer we've all been searching for? Can't we see it? Will somebody please say it!!? I can't get the words to describe what I'm feeling. I feel like the Grinch who's just given back Christmas. Only my heart has grown in the billions of times over. I have given Christmas back to those of you who receive this message. For Christmas is not about lavishing more toys on our children then they can even play with. Is it? Are we merely buying their smiles because we can no longer get them for ourselves with out appeasing their/our selfishness? This man who died believing he had the answer to all our troubles went against this principle and died for us to prove it. I think I'm going to heaven soon and I'm crying. It's one of those really bewildering heart wrenching cries down to your very core. The most heart wrenching cries you can ever get. You know the ones I speak of. You know? When some one calls you and tells you your mother has just past away. Any you had to leave her death bed to make more money. OH MY GOD! STOP TELLING ME. I DON'T WANT TO KNOW!!@! Have you had similar sorrows here on this world? Is this all of our hells combining to form one sick medley? Do you remember you first "true" love? Are you blessed enough to still have her? Do you remember what it felt like when you kissed her? Isn't that a true slice of heaven? Or when your baby is born? Isn't that the riches we really should be after? Really think about that. And once we all learn not to sin we all will be free to create a new planet. We can call it Eden or heaven2. Maybe when we all realize this we would all go to this place together in perfect harmony. Right on queue or is the cue... I'm crying again. I'm talking to myself. I'm talking to you. OH MY GOD!!! WHO AM I?!! Am I seeing what god is seeing? Are you seeing what god is seeing? Please, let's all not bury our head in the sand. Say we all, if educated to these beliefs and ideas and wonders still yet unexplored by we ignorant, greedy, selfish, lying, murderous, adulterous, and all together heartless or should I say soulless beings ever created in gods image, begin to live by the rules of common sense, humanity, religion, politics and which ever other way the want to divide you "people" and started living by the rules. How long would it take us to get to heaven? Oh my god. We must all be ready and able to sacrifice ourselves for the good of the whole, BUT WE MUST BE EXTREMELY RELUCTANT TO DO SO. Maybe our souls are freed when we can look and act toward on another as we were told to act, for our own well being as a whole society, not as individuals grabbing what we can while here on this planet, not as black or white, rich or poor, we'd all be about the same wealth because we would be looking for the real wealth in the rewards of a truly blissful exist we could create here. If we only took the examples god has been giving us and work together for the better good of us all. It's all for one or none at all. DONT YOU SEE THAT, YET?! It's right there in front of our faces but we are turning our backs on it. Stop this madness. Find your inner being and join me and many others on a truly miraculous journey to heaven. Here and in the other plain. Don't you get it? Please wake up. We don't have much time to act. They will surely silence me if they can? Wouldn't they want to? I believe I've seen why we are here. I believe a lot of you have seen it too. The Holy Spirit is the only way to describe what is making me feel these things. Have you all been aware of this answer and were keeping it from me until I discovered for myself? Now that I believe I know these answers will you take me to our leader? Or will you lock me up in a madhouse or jail or kill me or crucify me? You don't understand the power I now possess. You can threaten me with anything you want to. Take my money. Take my life or my/our/his children's lives or all my worldly possessions here on earth. Because I know this isn't heaven yet and I will get there no matter what you do to me here. Does everybody follow that "logic"? I don't believe I'm that frightened any more. I think I can get to heaven. I believe the best way for me to get there is to follow as many rules as I can. It's so scary yet I like it in some glorious way. PLEASE SEE IT WITH ME!!! I WANT YOU ALL THERE WITH ME!! Believe it or not we can still get there. You can all still get there. Just keep reading and sending this message around the world. Don't be so pessimistic. We are all made in his image. Remember this. IT'S TRUE!!

I'm crying again. This is my confession to the lord in case he takes me as I'm writing this. Oh my god!! I'm going mad. No, I'm not. I'm seeing this. And you're reading it as it's happening. You're with me!! You're writing this! All of your are!! Lord please forgive me for I have sinned. I've shunned my brothers all of them here on earth to better my material existence. I've committed adultery, stealing, lying. I've participated in abortion and have felt much guilt over it even before I truly received this message. I will work to right these wrongs. I'm still a bit scared yet. I think this is good. It may give me some time to think of what I'm truly beginning to see. It may give me time to truly cleanse my soul. I know other are waiting on the other side. I can feel them. Am I going mad? Or am I moving on to the next glorious plain? Please don't all be in a rush to follow me because you may not be ready, yet. But if you've received this message, hear/here then there may always be time for you to keep reading this message and find out what some one, some thing, some spirit is telling or coming to me and telling me to tell you people. I'm experiencing crying bouts as I write this and I'm begging whomever it is telling me this to go slowly. But no matter how painful it is for us to see this message we must truly see the error of our ways as a society, a world society. Oh my god. That's it. Don't you see? They are always threatening us with this one world mentality. Maybe we really should be striving for a one world. Don't we see the extremely hard times in ALL our futures on our present course? Do you think as a species we will be able to fend off all the natural and manmade catastrophes coming our way? With global warming and pollution already warming our planet to hellish temperatures? Where we are all stripping our home planet for money? When all the while object from space can be on their way to crush our tiny planet. And we are too busy defending ourselves from each other to stop and defend the entire world. HELLO PEOPLE!!! I'M NOT A GENIUS, BUT THAT DOESN'T MAKE MUCH SENSE TO ME!!! DOES IT TO YOU? People of the world, have aliens come down to take over our meager existence? Is this our god? Or did they come in peace and plant the seeds of good with in us all. Maybe there are aliens amongst us. Taking over or keeping control? Preying on our moral weaknesses? Maybe, if the message really gets out to the masses you will go out with this knowledge and seek the answers to correct the errors of our ways by uniting and helping each other. Oh my god. Are you aliens taking over this world or am I going to god. I must believe the latter. Oh my god, I'm still so, so scared. AM I worthy of your message? I apologize if this message rambles but it's not all of my doing. Things are popping in my head and heart. Please put in the news all the people doing good with their money. I for one can read this stuff all day long. But we need each other's help. We can not all find this answer together at the same time. OR CAN WE?! We must be diligent and patient in allowing all of us time to get the message, while still protecting our innocent form those that have not yet received it. Spread this word. Spread all good words like this. Become one of the mindless religious "nuts" who believe they've found the answer to a question more important then us all. IT IS THE SALVATION OF US ALL IN ALL its FORMS. DON'T WE ALL SEE THAT? Or just get the message that even common sense can only being you too. WE MUST FOLLOW THESE RULES OR WE WILL DESTROY OURSELVES. I've never read the bible/koran/torra or what ever you may use. I feel that I don't have to. I think I've gotten the TRUE AND REAL message. HAVE YOU?!! Now it is time for the ambitious to become the righteous. The righteous to fight to save the meek and for the meek to become the ambitious. Now sign your name for your part in this confession and repent with us. By doing so you will have signed your name in the book of eternal life.

LOVE

ME

George Clark

Light of the son

yeah, yeah, me too. I know I've been going about giving us all our medicine and made it taste awful too. Instead of coming in like a "lion" I guess I should have come like the lamb? I guess I'm going to have to join the pyramid scheme again, for my savior job just isn't paying the rent. I suppose jesus would want us to live under the all watching eye of those that live in pyramids? That's why he stood up and died for us. None of us are worthy of him and we shall reap the hell we have sowed because of it. At least I will know the real reason why we die at the hands of our brothers, the evil, or the aliens. I tried to frantically tell you of his message again and failed us all. I tried to whip you into submission because the lamb led gently and apparently he failed the good masses. I'm probably going to be losing my family soon for my madness of not wanting to play this losing game any longer. Why would I want to leave them where I was left off by those that killed christ by not following him? I'm sorry that I didn't receive the message before this world spoiled my soul with it's brother against brother creed.

I hope to find the love I once knew,

for that love was for all of you,

it now has turned to despair,

for I can see none whom care,

that the life that one gave,

for all of us to save,

was given in vain,

for our evil still remain,

the dominant power,

up until mankind's last evil hour,

when on bended knee,

they may all see,

the light of the son,

has finally won.

peace and I pray,

that at the end of this day,

you see that my sorrows,

was from seeing all our tomorrows,

that you think can't be fixed,

but that's merely the devil's trix,

for our path can always be bright,

if the good put up his fight,

by doing what is right.